HORRiD HENRY'S
Summer Fun

Francesca Simon spent her childhood on the beach
in California, and then went to Yale and Oxford
Universities to study medieval history and literature.
She now lives in London with her family. She has written
over 50 books and won the Children's Book of the Year
at the Galaxy British Book Awards for *Horrid Henry and
the Abominable Snowman*.

Tony Ross is one of the most popular and successful
of all children's illustrators, with almost 50 picture books
to his name. He has also produced line drawings for
many fiction titles, for authors such as David Walliams,
Enid Blyton, Astrid Lindgren and many more.

For a complete list of **Horrid Henry** titles
see the end of the book, or visit
www.horridhenry.co.uk
or
www.orionchildrensbooks.co.uk

HORRiD HENRY'S
Summer Fun

Francesca Simon
Illustrated by Tony Ross

Orion
Children's Books

ORION CHILDREN'S BOOKS
This collection first published in Great Britain in 2017
by Hodder and Stoughton
1 3 5 7 9 10 8 6 4 2

Text © Francesca Simon 1994, 1995, 1996,
2010, 2013, 2014, 2015, 2017
Illustrations © Tony Ross 1994, 1995, 1996,
2010, 2013, 2014, 2015, 2017
Puzzles and activities © Orion Children's Books, 2017

A CIP catalogue record for this book
is available from the British Library.

ISBN 978 1 5101 0216 3

Printed and bound in Great Britain by Clays Ltd, St Ives plc

The paper and board used in this book are from
well-managed forests and other responsible sources.

Orion Children's Books
An imprint of
Hachette Children's Books
Part of Hodder and Stoughton
Carmelite House
50 Victoria Embankment
London EC4Y 0DZ

An Hachette UK Company
www.hachette.co.uk
www.hachettechildrens.co.uk
www.horridhenry.co.uk

CONTENTS

HORRiD HENRY AND MOODY MARGARET

'I'm Captain Hook!'

'No, I'm Captain Hook!'

'I'm Captain Hook,' said Horrid
Henry.

'I'm Captain Hook,' said Moody
Margaret.

They glared at each other.

'It's *my* hook,' said Moody Margaret.

Moody Margaret lived next door.
She did not like Horrid Henry, and
Horrid Henry did not like her. But
when Rude Ralph was busy, Clever

Clare had flu, and Sour Susan was her
enemy, Margaret would jump over the
wall to play with Henry.

'Actually, it's my turn to be Hook
now,' said Perfect Peter. 'I've been the
prisoner for such a long time.'

'Prisoner, be quiet!'
said Henry.

'Prisoner, walk the
plank!' said Margaret.

'But I've walked
it fourteen times
already,' said Peter.
'Please can I be
Hook now?'

'No, by thunder!'
said Moody
Margaret. 'Now out of my way, worm!'
And she swashbuckled across the deck,
waving her hook and clutching her
sword and dagger.

Margaret had eyepatches and skulls
and crossbones and plumed hats and
cutlasses and sabres and snickersnees.

Henry had a stick. This was why
Henry played with Margaret.

But Henry had to do terrible things
before playing with Margaret's swords.
Sometimes he had to sit and wait while
she read a book. Sometimes he had
to play 'Mums and Dads' with her.

3

Worst of all (please don't tell anyone), sometimes he had to be the baby.

Henry never knew what Margaret would do.

When he put a spider on her arm, Margaret laughed.

When he pulled her hair, Margaret pulled his harder.

When Henry screamed, Margaret would scream louder. Or she would sing. Or pretend not to hear.

Sometimes Margaret was fun. But most of the time she was a moody old grouch.

'I won't play if I can't be Hook,' said Horrid Henry.

Margaret thought for a moment.

'We can both be Captain Hook,' she said.

'But we only have one hook,' said Henry.

'Which I haven't played with yet,' said Peter.

'BE QUIET, prisoner!' shouted Margaret. 'Mr Smee, take him to jail.'

'No,' said Henry.

'You will get your reward, Mr Smee,' said the Captain, waving her hook.

Mr Smee dragged the prisoner to the jail.

'If you're very quiet, prisoner, then you will be freed and you can be a pirate too,' said Captain Hook.

'Now give me the hook,' said Mr Smee. The Captain reluctantly handed it over.

'Now I'm Captain Hook and you're Mr Smee,' shouted Henry.

'I order everyone to walk the plank!'

'I'm sick of playing pirates,' said Margaret. 'Let's play something else.'

Henry was furious. That was just like Moody Margaret.

'Well, I'm playing pirates,' said Henry.

'Well I'm not,' said Margaret. 'Give me back my hook.'

'No,' said Henry.

Moody Margaret opened her mouth and screamed. Once Margaret started screaming she could go on and on and on.

Henry gave her the hook.

Margaret smiled.

'I'm hungry,' Margaret said. 'Got anything to eat?'

Henry had three bags of crisps and seven chocolate biscuits hidden in his room, but he certainly wasn't going to share them with Margaret.

'You can have a radish,' said Henry.

'What else?' said Margaret.

'A carrot,' said Henry.

'What else?' said Margaret.

'Glop,' said Henry.

'What's Glop?'

'Something special that only I can make,' said Henry.

'What's in it?' asked Margaret.

'That's a secret,' said Henry.

'I bet it's yucky,' said Margaret.

'Of course it's yucky,' said Henry.

'I can make the yuckiest Glop of all,' said Margaret.

'That's because you don't know anything. No one can make yuckier Glop than I can.'

'I dare you to eat Glop,' said Margaret.

'I double dare you back,' said Henry. 'Dares go first.'

Margaret stood up very straight.

'All right,' said Margaret. 'Glop starts with snails and worms.'

And she started poking under the bushes.

'Got one!' she shouted, holding up a fat snail. 'Now for some worms,' said Margaret.

She got down on her hands and knees and started digging a hole.

'You can't put anything from outside into Glop,' said Henry quickly. 'Only stuff in the kitchen.'

Margaret looked at Henry.

'I thought we were making Glop,' she said.

'We are,' said Henry. 'My way, because it's *my* house.'

Horrid Henry and Moody Margaret went into the gleaming white kitchen.

11

Henry got out two wooden mixing spoons and a giant red bowl.

'I'll start,' said Henry. He went to the cupboard and opened the doors wide.

'Porridge!' said Henry. And he poured some into the bowl.

Margaret opened the fridge and looked inside. She grabbed a small container.

'Soggy semolina!' shouted Margaret. Into the bowl it went.

'Coleslaw!'

'Spinach!'

'Coffee!'

'Yoghurt!'

'Flour!'

'Vinegar!'

'Baked beans!'

'Mustard!'

'Peanut butter!'

'Mouldy cheese!'

'Pepper!'

'Rotten oranges!'

'And ketchup!' shouted Henry.
He squirted in the ketchup until
the bottle was empty.

'Now, mix!' said
Margaret.

Horrid Henry
and Moody
Margaret
grabbed
hold of their
spoons with
both hands.

Then they plunged the spoons into the Glop and began to stir.

It was hard heavy work.

Faster and faster, harder and harder they stirred.

There was Glop on the ceiling. There was Glop on the floor. There was Glop on the clock, and Glop on the door. Margaret's hair was covered in Glop. So was Henry's face.

Margaret looked into the bowl. She had never seen anything so yucky in her life.

'It's ready,' she said.

Horrid Henry and Moody Margaret carried the Glop to the table.

Then they sat down and stared at the sloppy, slimey, sludgy, sticky, smelly, gooey, gluey, gummy, greasy, gloopy Glop.

'Right,' said Henry. 'Who's going to eat some first?'

There was a very long pause. Henry looked at Margaret. Margaret looked at Henry.

'Me,' said Margaret. 'I'm not scared.'

She scooped up a large spoonful and stuffed it in her mouth.

Then she swallowed. Her face went pink and purple and green.

'How does it taste?' said Henry.

'Good,' said Margaret, trying not to choke.

'Have some more then,' said Henry.

'Your turn first,' said Margaret.

Henry sat for a
moment and looked
at the Glop.

'My mum doesn't
like me to eat
between meals,' said
Henry.

'HENRY!' hissed
Moody Margaret.

Henry took a tiny
spoonful.

17

'More!' said Margaret.

Henry took a tiny bit more. The Glop wobbled lumpily on his spoon. It looked like . . . Henry did not want to think about what it looked like.

He closed his eyes and brought the spoon to his mouth.

'Ummm, yummm,' said Henry.

'You didn't eat any,' said Margaret. 'That's not fair.'

She scooped up some Glop and . . .

I dread to think what would have happened next, if they had not been interrupted.

'Can I come in now?' called a small voice from outside. 'It's my turn to be Hook.'

Horrid Henry had forgotten all about Perfect Peter.

'OK,' shouted Henry.

Peter came to the door.

'I'm hungry,' he said.

'Come in, Peter,' said Henry sweetly. 'Your dinner is on the table.'

Henry's Summer Howlers

Knock, knock.
Who's there?
Summer.
Summer who?
Summer better than
others at telling jokes.

What did the cake say
to the knife?
You wanna piece of me?

What happens when you throw a
yellow pebble into the blue sea?
It sinks.

Nitty Nora: Where do
nits go on holiday?
Henry: Search me

Which direction did the chicken swim
round the hotel pool?
Cluck-wise.

How do you know if it's raining?
Push your little brother outside and
see if he comes in wet.

Why didn't the elephant board his plane?
Because it wasn't a jumbo.

What is Greedy Graham's idea
of a balanced meal?
A banana sundae in one hand and
a strawberry sundae in the other.

FLUFFY STRUTS HER STUFF

'Fluffy. Fetch,' said Perfect Peter.

Snore.

'Fluffy. Fetch!' said Perfect Peter.

Snore.

'Go on, Fluffy,' said Perfect Peter, dangling a squeaky toy tarantula in front of the snoozing cat. 'Fetch!'

Fat Fluffy stretched.

Yawn.

Snore. Snore.

'What *are* you doing, worm?' said Horrid Henry.

Peter jumped. Should he tell Henry about his brilliant idea? What if Henry copied him? That would be just like Henry. Well, let him try, thought Peter. Fluffy is my cat.

'I'm training Fluffy for Scruffs,' said Peter. 'She's sure to win this year.'

Scruffs was the annual neighbourhood pet show. Last year Henry had spent one of the most boring days of his life watching horrible dogs compete for who looked the most like their owner, or who had the waggiest tail or fluffiest coat.

Horrid Henry snorted.

'Which category?' said
Henry. 'Ugliest Owner?
Fattest Cat?'

'*Most Obedient*,'
said Peter.

Horrid Henry
snorted
again. Trust
his worm toad nappy face
brother to come
up with such a
dumb idea.

Fat Fluffy was the
world's most useless cat.
Fluffy did
nothing but
eat and sleep
and snore. She
was so lazy that
Horrid Henry was shocked
every time she moved.

25

Squeak! Perfect Peter waved the rubber tarantula in front of Fluffy's face. He knew Henry would make fun of him. Well, this time he, Peter, would have the last laugh. He would show the world what an amazing cat Fluffy was, and no one, especially Henry, could stop him. Peter knew that Fluffy had hidden greatness. After all, thought Peter, not everyone knows how clever I am. The same was true of Fluffy.

'Fluffy, when I squeak this toy, you sit up and give me your paw,' said Peter. 'When I squeak it twice, you roll over.'

'You can't train a cat, toad,' said Henry.

'Yes, I can,' said Peter. 'And don't call me toad.' What did Henry know, anyway? Nothing. Peter had seen dogs herding sheep. Jumping through hoops. Even dancing.

True, they had all been dogs, and Fluffy was a cat. But she was no ordinary cat.

Horrid Henry smirked.

'Okay Peter, because I'm such a nice brother I'll show you how to train Fluffy,' said Henry.

'Can you really?' said Peter.

'Yup,' said Henry. 'When I give the command, Fluffy will do exactly what I say.'

So far that was more than Peter had managed. A lot more.

'And it will only cost you £1,' said Henry.

Well, it was definitely worth a pound if it meant Fluffy could win Most Obedient.

Peter handed over the money.

"Now watch and learn, worm," said Horrid Henry. "Fluffy. Sleep!"

Fluffy slept.

"See?" said Henry. "She obeyed."

Perfect Peter was outraged.

"That doesn't count," said Peter. "I want my money back."

"You can't have it," said Henry. "I did exactly what I said I would do."

"Mum!" wailed Peter. "Henry tricked me."

"Shut up, toad," said Horrid Henry.

"Mum! Henry told me to shut up," screamed Peter.

"Henry! Don't be horrid," shouted Mum.

Horrid Henry wasn't listening. He was an idiot. He had just had the most brilliant, spectacular idea. He could train Fluffy *and* play the best ever trick on

28

Peter in the history of the world. No, the universe. That would pay Peter back for getting Henry into such big trouble over breaking Mum's camera. One day, thought Horrid Henry, he would write a famous book collecting all his best tricks, and sell it for a million pounds a copy. Parliament would declare a special holiday – *Henry Day* – to celebrate his brilliance. There would be street parties

and parades in his honour. The Queen
would knight him. But until then . . . he
had work to do.

Horrid Henry gave Peter back his
£1 coin.

Perfect Peter was amazed. Henry
never handed back money voluntarily.
He looked at the coin suspiciously. Had
Henry substituted a plastic pound coin
like the last time?

'That was just a joke,' said Henry
smoothly. 'Of course I can train Fluffy
for you.'

'How?' said Peter. He'd been trying
for days.

'That's my secret,' said Henry. 'But
I am so confident I can do it I'll even
give you a money-back guarantee.'

A money-back guarantee! That
sounded almost too good to be true.
In fact . . .

'Is this a trick?' said Peter.

'No!' said Henry. 'Out of the goodness of my heart, I offer to spend my valuable time training your cat. I'm

insulted. Just for that I won't—'

'Okay,' said Peter. 'How much?'

Yes! thought Horrid Henry.

'£5,' said Henry.

'£5!' gasped Peter.

'That's a bargain,' said Henry, 'Not everyone can train a cat. Okay, £5 money-back guarantee that Fluffy will obey four commands in time for Scruffs.

If not, you'll get your money back.'

How could he lose? thought Peter.

'Deal,' he said.

Yes! thought Horrid Henry.

Somehow he didn't think he'd have too much trouble training Fluffy to Stay. Sleep. Breathe. Snore. No trouble at all.

Perfect Peter bounced up and down with

excitement. Today was the big day.
Today was the day when he took Fluffy
to win Most Obedient pet at Scruffs.

'Shouldn't I practise with her?' said
Peter.

'No!' said Henry quickly. 'Cats are
tricky. You only get one chance to make
them obey, so we need to save it for the
judge.'

'Okay, Henry,' said Peter. After all,
Henry had given him a money-back
guarantee.

Greedy Graham was at the park with
his enormous guinea pig,
Fattie. Rude Ralph
had brought his
mutt, Windbag,
who was
competing for
Waggiest Tail.

Sour Susan was there with her pug, Grumpy. Aerobic Al was there with his greyhound, Speedy. Lazy Linda's

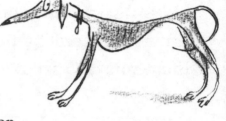

rabbit, Snore, dozed on her shoulder. Even Miss Lovely had brought her

Yorkie, Baby Jane. There were pets everywhere.

'What's your dog called, Bert?' said Henry.

'I dunno,' said Beefy Bert.

'Waaah,' wailed Weepy William. 'Mr Socks didn't win the Fluffiest Kitty contest.'

'Piddle. Sit!' came a familiar, steely voice, like a jagged knife being dragged across a boulder.

Horrid Henry gasped.

There was Miss Battle-Axe, walking beside the most groomed dog Henry had ever seen. The poodle was covered in ribbons and fancy collars and velvet bows.

He watched as Miss Battle-Axe found a quiet corner and put on some music.

Boom-chick boom-chick boom-chick-boom!

Miss Battle-Axe danced around Piddle.

She clicked her fingers.

Piddle danced around Miss Battle-Axe.

Miss Battle-Axe danced backwards, waving her arms and clicking again.

Piddle danced backwards.

Miss Battle-Axe danced forwards, hopping. Piddle danced forwards.

Double click. Miss Battle-Axe danced off to the left. Piddle danced off to the right. Then they met back at the centre.

Finally, Miss Battle-Axe crouched, and Piddle jumped over her.

'Wow,' said Perfect Peter, glancing at Fat Fluffy snoring on the grass. 'Do you think we could teach Fluffy to do tricks like that?'

'Already have,' said Horrid Henry.

Peter gazed at Henry open-mouthed.

'Really?' said Peter.

'Yup,' said Henry. 'Just squeeze the tarantula and tell Fluffy what you want her to do.'

'Line up here for Most Obedient pet,' said the organiser.

'That's me!' said Peter.

ZZZZZ

'All you have to remember, one squeak to make Fluffy sit up, two squeaks to make her walk on her hind legs,' said Henry as they stood in the queue. 'Three squeaks will make her come running to you.'

'Okay, Henry,' said Peter.

Tee hee.

Revenge was sweet, thought Horrid Henry. Wouldn't Peter look an idiot trying to give orders to a cat? And naturally he'd find a way to keep Peter's £5.

Peter handed in his entry ticket at the enclosure's entrance.

'Sorry, your brother's too young,' said the man at the gate. 'You'll have to show the cat.'

Horrid Henry froze with horror.

'Me?' said Horrid Henry. 'But . . . but
. . .'

'But she's my cat,' said Perfect Peter.
'I—'

'Come along, come along, we're about
to start,' said the man, shoving Henry
and Fat Fluffy into the ring.

Horrid Henry found himself standing
in the centre. He had the only cat.
Everyone was staring and pointing and
laughing. Oh, where was a cloak of
invisibility when you needed one?

'Put your pets through their paces now,' shouted the judge.

All the dogs started to Sit. Stay. Come. Fetch. Piddle the poodle began to dance.

Fluffy lay curled in a ball at Henry's feet.

'Stay!' said Horrid Henry as the judge walked by.

Maybe he could get Fluffy at least to sit up. Or even just move a bit.

Horrid Henry squeezed the tarantula toy.

Squeak!

'Come on, Fluffy. Move!'

Fluffy didn't even raise her

40

head.

Squeak! Squeak! Squeak!

'Fluffy. Wake up!'

Aerobic Al's dog began
to bark.

Horrid Henry squeezed the tarantula
toy again.

Squeak! Squcak!

Piddle stood on his hind legs and
danced in a circle.

'No, Piddle,' hissed Miss Battle-Axe, gesturing wildly, 'turn to the right.'

'Fluffy. Sit!' said Horrid Henry.

Squeak! Squeak!

Babbling Bob's mutt started growling.

Come on, Fluffy, thought Horrid Henry desperately, squeezing the toy in front of the dozing cat. 'Do something. Anything.'

Squeeeeeak. Squeeeeeeak! Squeeeeeeeeeeeak!

Piddle ran over and peed on the judge's leg.

'Piddle,' squawked Miss Battle-Axe. 'NO!'

Squeak! Squeak! Squeak!

Sour Susan's dog Grumpy bit the dog next to him.

Horrid Henry waved his arms. 'Come on, Fluffy. You can do it!'

ZZZZZ

Weepy William's dog started running
in circles.

'Piddle! Come back!' shrieked Miss
Battle-Axe as Piddle ran from the ring,

howling. Every
other dog chased
after him, barking
and yelping, their
owners running after
them screaming.

The only animal left
was Fat Fluffy.

'Fluffy. Stay!' ordered
Horrid Henry.

Snore.
Snore. Snore.

'The cat's the
winner,' said the
judge.

'Yippee!' screamed Perfect
Peter. 'I knew you
could do it, Fluffy!'

'Meow.'

Henry's Summer Howlers

What makes the Tower
of Pisa lean?
It doesn't eat much.

What do jelly babies
wear in the rain?
Gum boots.

What colour is the wind?
Blew.

Henry's Dad: Are the rooms here quiet?
*Hotel manager: Yes, sir, it's only the guests
that are noisy.*

Knock, knock.
Who's there?
Felix.
Felix who?
Felix my ice-cream,
I'll lick his.

What do horses suffer
from in the summertime?
Neigh fever.

Why can't you starve in the desert?
Because of the sand which is there.

Why was Miss Battle-
Axe's poodle, Piddle,
excited?
*Because she was going
on her howl-idays.*

HORRID HENRY'S WEDDING

'I'm not wearing these horrible clothes and that's that!'

Horrid Henry glared at the mirror. A stranger smothered in a lilac ruffled shirt, green satin knickerbockers, tights, pink cummerbund tied in a floppy bow and pointy white satin shoes with gold buckles glared back at him.

Henry had never seen anyone looking so silly in his life.

'Aha ha ha ha ha!' shrieked Horrid Henry, pointing at the mirror.

Then Henry peered more closely. The ridiculous looking boy was him.

Perfect Peter stood next to Horrid Henry. He too was smothered in a lilac ruffled shirt, green satin knickerbockers, tights, pink cummerbund and pointy white shoes with gold buckles. But unlike Henry, Peter was smiling.

'Aren't they adorable?' squealed Prissy Polly. 'That's how my children are always going to dress.'

Prissy Polly was Horrid Henry's horrible older cousin. Prissy Polly was always squeaking and squealing:

'Eeek, it's a speck of dust.'

'Eeek, it's a puddle.'

'Eeek, my hair is a mess.'

But when Prissy Polly announced she was getting married to Pimply Paul and wanted Henry and Peter to be pageboys, Mum said yes, before Henry could stop her.

'What's a pageboy?' asked Henry suspiciously.

'A pageboy carries the wedding rings down the aisle on a satin cushion,' said Mum.

'And throws confetti afterwards,' said Dad.

Henry liked the idea of throwing confetti. But carrying rings on a cushion? No thanks.

'I don't want to be a pageboy,' said Henry.

'I do, I do,' said Peter.

'You're going to be a pageboy, and that's that,' said Mum.

'And you'll behave yourself,' said Dad. 'It's very kind of cousin Polly to ask you.'

Henry scowled.

'Who'd want to be married to *her*?'

said Henry. 'I wouldn't if you paid me a million pounds.'

But for some reason the bridegroom, Pimply Paul, did want to marry Prissy Polly. And as far as Henry knew, he had not been paid one million pounds.

Pimply Paul was also trying on his wedding clothes. He looked ridiculous in a black top hat, lilac shirt, and a black jacket covered in gold swirls.

'I won't wear these silly clothes,' said Henry.

'Oh be quiet, you little brat,' snapped Pimply Paul.

Horrid Henry glared at him.

'I won't,' said Henry. 'And that's final.'

'Henry, stop being horrid,' said Mum. She looked extremely silly in a big floppy hat dripping with flowers.

Suddenly Henry grabbed at the lace ruffles round his throat.

'I'm choking,' he gasped, 'I can't breathe.'

Then Henry fell to the floor and rolled around.

'Ugggggghhhhhhh,' moaned Henry. 'I'm dying.'

'Get up this minute, Henry!' said Dad.

'Eeek, there's dirt on the floor!'
shrieked Polly.

'Can't you control that child?' hissed
Pimply Paul.

'I DON'T WANT TO BE A
PAGEBOY!' howled Horrid Henry.

'Thank you so much for asking me to
be a pageboy, Polly,' shouted Perfect
Peter, trying to be heard over Henry's
screams.

'You're welcome,' shouted Polly.

'Stop that, Henry!' ordered Mum.
'I've never been so ashamed in my life.'

'I hate children,' muttered Pimply
Paul under his breath.

Horrid Henry stopped.
Unfortunately, his pageboy clothes
looked as fresh and crisp as ever.

All right, thought Horrid Henry. You
want me at the wedding? You've got
me.

★

Prissy Polly's wedding day arrived. Henry was delighted to see rain pouring down. How cross Polly would be.

Perfect Peter was already dressed.

'Isn't this going to be fun, Henry?' said Peter.

'No!' said Henry, sitting on the floor. 'And I'm not going.'

Mum and Dad stuffed Henry into his pageboy clothes. It was hard, heavy work. Finally everyone was in the car.

'We're going to be late!' shrieked Mum.

'We're going to be late!' shrieked Dad.

'We're going to be late!' shrieked Perfect Peter.

'Good!' muttered Henry.

Mum, Dad, Henry and Peter arrived at the church. Boom! There was a clap of thunder. Rain poured down. All the other guests were already inside.

'Watch out for the puddle, boys,' said
Mum, as she leapt out of the car. She
opened her umbrella.

Dad jumped over the puddle.

Peter jumped over the puddle.

Henry jumped over the puddle, and
tripped.

SPLASH!

'Oopsy,' said Henry.

His ruffles were torn, his knickerbockers were filthy, and his satin shoes were soaked.

Mum, Dad and Peter were covered in muddy water.

Perfect Peter burst into tears.

'You've ruined my pageboy clothes,' sobbed Peter.

Mum wiped as much dirt as she could off Henry and Peter.

'It was an accident, Mum, really,' said Henry.

'Hurry up, you're late!' shouted Pimply Paul.

Mum and Dad dashed into the church. Henry and Peter stayed outside, waiting to make their entrance.

Pimply Paul and his best man, Cross Colin, stared at Henry and Peter.

'You look a mess,' said Paul.

'It was an accident,' said Henry.

Peter snivelled.

'Now be careful with the wedding rings,' said Cross Colin. He handed Henry and Peter a satin cushion each, with a gold ring on top.

A great quivering lump of lace and taffeta and bows and flowers approached. Henry guessed Prissy Polly must be lurking somewhere underneath.

'Eeek,' squeaked the clump. 'Why did it have to rain on my wedding?'

'Eeek,' squeaked the clump again. 'You're filthy.'

Perfect Peter began to sob. The satin cushion trembled in his hand. The ring balanced precariously near the edge.

Cross Colin snatched Peter's cushion. 'You can't carry a ring with your hand shaking like that,'snapped Colin. 'You'd better carry them both, Henry.'

'*Come on,*' hissed Pimply Paul. 'We're late!'

Cross Colin and Pimply Paul dashed into the church.

The music started. Henry pranced down the aisle after Polly. Everyone stood up.

Henry beamed and bowed and waved. He was King Henry the Horrible, smiling graciously at his cheering subjects before he chopped off their heads.

As he danced along, he stepped on Polly's long trailing dress.

Riiiiip

'Eeeeek!' squeaked Prissy Polly.

Part of Polly's train lay beneath Henry's muddy satin shoe.

That dress was too long anyway, thought Henry. He picked the fabric out of the way and stomped down the aisle.

The bride, groom, best man, and pageboys assembled in front of the minister.

Henry stood ... and stood ... and stood. The minister droned on ... and on ... and on. Henry's arm holding up the cushion began to ache.

This is boring, thought Henry, jiggling the rings on the cushion.

Boing! Boing! Boing!

Oooh, thought Henry. I'm good at ring tossing.

The rings bounced.

The minister droned.

Henry was a famous pancake chef, tossing the pancakes higher and higher and higher...

Clink clunk.

The rings rolled down the aisle and vanished down a small grate.

Oops, thought Henry.

'May I have the rings, please?' said the
minister.

Everyone looked at Henry.

'He's got them,' said Henry
desperately, pointing at Peter.

'I have not,' sobbed Peter.

Henry reached into his pocket. He found two pieces of old chewing-gum, some gravel, and his lucky pirate ring.

'Here, use this,' he said.

At last, Pimply Paul and Prissy Polly were married.

Cross Colin handed Henry and Peter a basket of pink and yellow rose petals each.

'Throw the petals in front of the bride and groom as they walk back down the aisle,' whispered Colin.

'I will,' said Peter. He scattered the petals before Pimply Paul and Prissy Polly.

'So will I,' said Henry. He hurled a handful of petals in Pimply Paul's face.

'Watch it, you little brat,' snarled Paul.

'Windy, isn't it?' said Henry. He hurled another handful of petals at Polly.

'Eeek,' squeaked Prissy Polly.

'Everyone outside for photographs,' said the photographer.

Horrid Henry loved having his picture taken. He dashed out.

'Pictures of the bride and groom first,' said the photographer.

Henry jumped in front.

Click.

Henry peeked from the side.

Click.

Henry stuck out his tongue.

Click.

Henry made horrible rude faces.

Click.

'This way to the reception!' said Cross Colin.

The wedding party was held in a nearby hotel.

The adults did nothing but talk and eat, talk and drink, talk and eat.

Perfect Peter sat at the table and ate his lunch.

Horrid Henry sat under the table and poked people's legs. He crawled around and squashed some toes. Then Henry got bored and drifted into the next room.

There was the wedding cake, standing alone, on a table. It was the most delicious-looking cake Henry had ever seen. It had three layers and was covered in luscious white icing and yummy iced flowers and bells and leaves.

Henry's mouth watered.

I'll just taste a teeny weeny bit of petal, thought Henry. No harm in that.

He broke off a morsel and popped it in his mouth.

Hmmmmm boy! That icing tasted great.

Perhaps just one more bite, thought
Henry. If I take it from the back, no
one will notice.

Henry carefully selected an icing rose
from the bottom tier and stuffed it in
his mouth. Wow.

Henry stood back from the cake.
It looked a little uneven now, with that
rose missing from the bottom.

I'll just even it up, thought Henry.
It was the work of a moment to break
off a rose from the middle tier and
another from the top.

Then a strange thing happened.

'Eat me,' whispered the cake. 'Go
on.'

Who was Henry to ignore such a
request?

He picked out a few crumbs from the
back.

Delicious, thought Henry. Then he took a few more. And a few more. Then he dug out a nice big chunk.

'What do you think you're doing?' shouted Pimply Paul.

Henry ran round the cake table. Paul ran after him.

Round and round and round the cake they ran.

'Just wait till I get my hands on you!' snarled Pimply Paul.

Henry dashed under the table. Pimply Paul lunged for him and missed.

SPLAT!

Pimply Paul fell head first on to the cake.

Prissy Polly ran into the room.

'Eeek,' she shrieked.

★

'Wasn't that a lovely wedding,' sighed Mum on the way home. 'Funny they didn't have a cake, though.'

'Oh yes,' said Dad.

'Oh yes,' said Peter.

'Oh yes!' said Henry. 'I'll be glad to be a pageboy anytime.'

Henry's Summer Howlers

Why is the letter T like an island? Because it's in the middle of water.

What did the computer do at the beach? It put on screensaver and surfed the net.

Why did Clever Clare do her homework on the aeroplane? She wanted a higher education.

Where do you learn how
to make ice cream?
Sundae school.

How is the sea held in place?
It's tied.

Where do ghosts
go on holiday?
Death Valley

Why do seagulls live on the beach?
If they lived by the bay they'd be bagels.

How do you stop someone
who's been working out in the gym
on a hot day from smelling?
Put a peg on his nose.

MOODY MARGARET'S SLEEPOVER

'What are you doing here?' said Moody Margaret, glaring.

'I'm here for the sleepover,' said Sour Susan, glaring back.

'You were uninvited, remember?' said Margaret.

'And then you invited me again, remember?' snapped Susan.

'Did not.'

'Did too. You told me last week I could come!'

'Didn't.'

71

'Did. You're such a meanie,
Margaret,' scowled Susan. Aaaarrggghh.
Why was she friends with such a moody
old grouch?

Moody Margaret heaved a heavy sigh.
Why was she friends with such a sour
old slop bucket?

'Well, since you're here, I guess you'd
better come in,' said Margaret. 'But don't
expect any dessert 'cause there won't be
enough for you and my *real* guests.'

Sour Susan stomped inside Margaret's
house. Grrrr. She wouldn't be inviting
Margaret to her next sleepover party,
that's for sure.

★

Horrid Henry couldn't sleep. He was
hot. He was hungry.

'Biscuits!' moaned his tummy. 'Give
me biscuits!'

Because Mum
and Dad were the
meanest, most
horrible parents in
the world, they'd
forgotten to buy
more biscuits and

there wasn't a single solitary crumb in
the house. Henry knew because he'd
searched everywhere.

'Give me biscuits!' growled his
tummy. 'What are you waiting for?'

I'm going to die of hunger up here,
thought Horrid Henry. And it will be
all Mum and Dad's fault. They'll come
in tomorrow morning and find just a
few wisps of hair and some teeth. Then
they'd be sorry. Then they'd wail and
gnash. But it would be too late.

'How could we have forgotten to buy
chocolate biscuits?' Dad would sob.

'We deserve to be locked up forever!'
Mum would shriek.

'And now there's nothing left of
Henry but a tooth, and it's all our fault!'
they'd howl.

Humph. Serve them right.

Wait. What an idiot he was. Why
should he risk death from starvation
when he knew where there was a rich
stash of all sorts of yummy biscuits
waiting just for him?

Moody Margaret's Secret Club tent
was sure to be full to bursting with

goodies! Horrid Henry hadn't raided it in ages. And so long as he was quick, no one would ever know he'd left the house.

'Go on, Henry,' urged his tummy. 'FEED ME!'

Horrid Henry didn't need to be urged twice.

Slowly, quietly, he sneaked out of bed, crept down the stairs, and tiptoed out of the back door. Then quick over the wall, and hey presto, he was in the Secret Club tent. There was Margaret's Secret Club biscuit tin, in her pathetic hiding place under a blanket. Ha!

Horrid Henry prised open the lid. Oh wow. It was filled to the brim with Chocolate Fudge Chewies! And those scrumptious Triple Chocolate Chip

Marshmallow Squidgies! Henry scooped up a huge handful and stuffed them in his mouth.

Chomp. Chomp. Chomp.

Oh wow. Oh wow. Was there anything more delicious in the whole wide world than a mouthful of nicked biscuits?

'More! More! More!' yelped his tummy.

Who was Horrid Henry to say no?

Henry reached in to snatch another mega handful . . .

BANG! SLAM! BANG!

STOMP! STOMP! STOMP!

'That's too bad, Gurinder,' snapped Margaret's voice. 'It's my party so I decide. Hurry up, Susan.'

'I am hurrying,' said Susan's voice.

The footsteps were heading straight for the Secret Club tent.

Yikes. What was Margaret doing outside at this time of night? There wasn't a moment to lose.

Horrid Henry looked around wildly. Where could he hide? There was a wicker chest at the back, where Margaret kept her dressing-up clothes. Horrid Henry leapt inside and pulled the lid shut. Hopefully, the girls wouldn't be long and he could escape home before Mum and Dad discovered he'd been out.

Moody Margaret bustled into the
tent, followed by her mother, Gorgeous
Gurinder, Kung-Fu Kate, Lazy Linda,
Vain Violet, Singing Soraya and Sour
Susan.

'Now, girls, it's late, I want you to go
straight to bed, lights out, no talking,'
said Margaret's mother. 'My little Maggie
Moo Moo needs her beauty sleep.'

Ha, thought Horrid Henry. Margaret
could sleep for a thousand years and
she'd still look like a frog.

'Yes, Mum,' said Margaret.

'Good night, girls,' trilled Margaret's mum. 'See you in the morning.'

Phew, thought Horrid Henry, lying as still as he could. He'd be back home in no time, mission safely accomplished.

'We're sleeping out here?' said Singing Soraya. 'In a tent?'

'I said it was a Secret Club sleepover,' said Margaret.

Horrid Henry's heart sank. Huh? They were planning to sleep here? Rats rats rats double rats. He was going to have to hide inside this hot dusty trunk until they were asleep.

Maybe they'd all fall asleep soon, thought Horrid Henry hopefully.

Because he had to get home before Mum and Dad discovered he was missing. If they realised he'd sneaked outside, he'd be in so much trouble his life wouldn't be worth living and he might as well abandon all hope of ever watching TV or eating another biscuit until he was an old, shrivelled bag of bones struggling to chew with his one tooth and watch telly with his magnifying glass and hearing aid. Yikes!

Horrid Henry looked grimly at the biscuits clutched in his fist. Thank goodness he'd brought provisions. He might be trapped here for a very long time.

'Where's your sleeping bag, Violet?' said Margaret.

'I didn't bring one,' said Vain Violet. 'I don't like sleeping on the floor.'

'Tough,' said Margaret, 'that's where we're sleeping.'

'But I need to sleep in a bed,' whined Vain Violet. 'I don't want to sleep out here.'

'Well we do,' said Margaret.

'Yeah,' said Susan.

'I can sleep anywhere,' said Lazy Linda, yawning.

'I'm calling my mum,' said Violet. 'I want to go home.'

'Go ahead,' said Margaret. 'We don't

need you, do we?'

Silence.

'Oh go on, Violet, stay,' said
Gurinder.

'Yeah, stay,' said Kung-Fu Kate.

'No!' said Violet, flouncing out of the
tent.

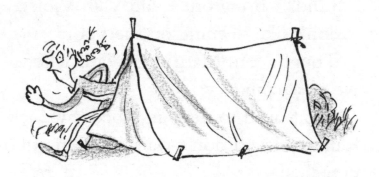

'Hummph,' said Moody Margaret.
'She's no fun anyway. Now, everyone
put your sleeping bags down where I
say. I need to sleep by the entrance,
because I need fresh air.'

'I want to sleep by the entrance,' said
Soraya.

'No,' said Margaret, 'it's my party so I decide. Susan, you go at the back because you snore.'

'Do not,' said Susan.

'Do too,' said Margaret.

'Liar.'

'Liar.'

SLAP!

SLAP!

'That's it!' wailed Susan. 'I'm calling my mum.'

'Go ahead,' said Margaret, 'see if I care, snore-box. That'll be loads more Chocolate Fudge Chewies for the rest of us.'

Sour Susan stood still. She'd been looking forward to Margaret's sleepover for ages. And she still hadn't had any of the midnight feast Margaret had promised.

'All right, I'll stay,' said Susan sourly, putting her sleeping bag down at the back of the tent by the dressing-up chest.

'I want to be next to Gurinder,' said Lazy Linda, scratching her head.

'Do you have nits?' said Gurinder.

'No!' said Linda.

'You do too,' said Gurinder.

'Do not,' said Linda.

'Do too,' said Gurinder. 'I'm not sleeping next to someone who has nits.'

'Me neither,' said Kate.

'Me neither,' said Soraya.

'Don't look at me,' said Margaret. 'I'm not sleeping next to you.'

'I don't have nits!' wailed Linda.

'Go next to Susan,' said Margaret.

'But she snores!' protested Linda.

'But she has nits!' protested Susan.

'Do not.'

'Do not.'

'Nitty!'

'Snory!'

Suddenly something scuttled across the floor.

'EEEEK!' squealed Soraya. 'It's a mouse!' She scrambled onto the dressing-up chest. The lid sagged.

'It won't hurt you,' said Margaret.

'Yeah,' said Susan.

'Eeeek!' squcaled Linda, shrinking back.

The lid sagged even more.

Cree—eaaak went the chest.

Aaarrrrggghhh, thought Horrid

Henry, trying to squash himself down
before he was squished.

'Eeeek!' squealed Gurinder, scrambling
onto the chest.

CREE—EAAAAAK! went the chest.

Errrrgh, thought Horrid Henry,
pushing up against the sagging lid as
hard as he could.

'I can't sleep if there's a . . . mouse,'
said Gurinder. She looked around
nervously. 'What if it runs on top of my
sleeping bag?'

Margaret sighed. 'It's only a mouse,' she said.

'I'm scared of mice,' whimpered Gurinder. 'I'm leaving!' And she ran out of the tent, wailing.

'More food for the rest of us,' said Margaret, shrugging. 'I say we feast now.'

'About time,' said Soraya.

'Let's start with the Chocolate Fudge Chewies,' said Margaret, opening the Secret Club biscuit tin. 'Everyone can have two, except for me, I get four 'cause it's my . . .'

Margaret peered into the tin. There were only a few crumbs inside.

'Who stole the biscuits?' said Margaret.

'Wasn't me,' said Susan.

'Wasn't me,' said Soraya.

'Wasn't me,' said Kate.

'Wasn't me,' said Linda.

Tee hee, thought Horrid Henry.

'One of you did, so no one is getting anything to eat until you admit it,' snapped Margaret.

'Meanie,' muttered Susan sourly.

'What did you say?' said Moody Margaret.

'Nothing,' said Susan.

'Then we'll just have to wait for the culprit to come forward,' said Margaret, scowling. 'Meanwhile, get in your sleeping bags. We're going to tell scary stories in the dark. Who knows a good one?'

'I do,' said Susan.

'Not the story about the ghost kitty-cat which drank up all the milk in your kitchen, is it?' said Margaret.

Susan scowled.

'Well, it's a true scary story,' said Susan.

'I know a real scary story,' said
Kung-Fu Kate. 'It's about this
monster—'

'Mine's better,' said Margaret. 'It's
about a flesh-eating zombie which
creeps around at night and rips off—'

'NOOOO,' wailed Linda. 'I hate
being scared. I'm calling my mum to
come and get me.'

'No scaredy-cats allowed in the Secret Club,' said Margaret.

'I don't care,' said Linda, flouncing out.

'It's not a sleepover unless we tell ghost stories,' said Moody Margaret. 'Turn off your torches. It won't be scary unless we're all sitting in the dark.'

Sniffle. Sniffle. Sniffle.

'I want to go home,' snivelled Soraya. 'I've never slept away from home before . . . I want my mummy.'

'What a baby,' said Moody Margaret.

★

Horrid Henry was cramped and hot and uncomfortable. Pins and needles were shooting up his arm. He shifted his shoulder, brushing against the lid.

There was a muffled creak.

Henry froze. Whoops. Henry prayed they hadn't heard anything.

'. . . and the zombie crept inside
the tent gnashing its bloody teeth and
sniffing the air for human flesh, hungry
for more—'

Ow. His poor aching arm. Henry
shifted position again.

Creak . . .

'What was that?' whispered Susan.

'What was what?' said Margaret.

'There was a . . . a . . . creak . . .' said
Susan.

'The wind,' said Margaret. 'Anyway,
the zombie sneaked into the tent and—'

'You don't think . . .' hissed Kate.

'Think what?' said Margaret.

'That the zombie . . . the zombie . . .'

I'm starving, thought Horrid Henry.
I'll just eat a few biscuits really, really,
really quietly—

Crunch. Crunch.

'What was that?' whispered Susan.

'What was what?' said Margaret.
'You're ruining the story!'

'That . . . crunching sound,' hissed
Susan.

Horrid Henry gasped. What an idiot
he was! Why hadn't he thought of this
before?

Crunch. Crunch. Crunch.

'Like someone . . . someone . . .
crunching on . . . bones,' whispered
Kung-Fu Kate.

'Someone . . . here . . .' whispered
Susan.

Tap. Horrid Henry rapped on the
underside of the lid.

Tap! Tap! Tap!

'I didn't hear anything,' said Margaret
loudly.

'It's the zombie!' screamed Susan.

'He's in here!' screamed Kate.

AAAAARRRRRRRGHHHHHHH!'

'I'm going home!' screamed Susan and
Kate. 'MUUUUUUMMMMMMY!'

Ha ha, thought Horrid Henry. His
brilliant plan had worked!!! Tee hee.
He'd hop out, steal the rest of the feast
and scoot home. Hopefully Mum and
Dad—

YANK!

Suddenly the chest lid was flung open and a torch shone in his eyes. Moody Margaret's hideous face glared down at him.

'Gotcha!' said Moody Margaret. 'Oh boy, are you in trouble. Just wait 'til I tell on you. Ha ha, Henry, you're dead.'

Horrid Henry climbed out of the chest and brushed a few crumbs onto the carpet.

'Just wait till I tell everyone at school about your sleepover,' said Horrid

Henry. 'How you were so mean and bossy everyone ran away.'

'Your parents will punish you forever,' said Moody Margaret.

'Your name will be mud forever,' said Horrid Henry. 'Everyone will laugh at you and serves you right, Maggie Moo Moo.'

'Don't call me that,' said Margaret, glaring.

'Call you what, Moo Moo?'

'All right,' said Margaret slowly. 'I won't tell on you if you give me two packs of Chocolate Fudge Chewies.'

'No way,' said Henry. 'I won't tell on you if you give me three packs of Chocolate Fudge Chewies.'

'Fine,' said Margaret. 'Your parents are still up, I'll tell them where you are right now. I wouldn't want them to worry.'

'Go ahead,' said Henry. 'I can't wait until school tomorrow.'

Margaret scowled.

'Just this once,' said Horrid Henry. 'I won't tell on you if you won't tell on me.'

'Just this once,' said Moody Margaret. 'But never again.'

They glared at each other.

When he was king, thought Horrid Henry, anyone named Margaret would be catapulted over the walls into an

oozy swamp. Meanwhile . . . on guard,
Margaret. On guard. I will be avenged!

Henry's Summer Howlers

Why should Sports Day
never be held in the jungle?
There are too many cheetahs.

Knock, knock.
Who's there?
Ice cream soda.
Ice cream soda who?
ICE CREAM SODA
PEOPLE CAN HEAR ME . . .

Why did the elephant cross the road?
The chicken was on
her summer holidays.

What does the
Spanish farmer say
to his chickens?
'Oh lay!'

Why is it always hot in a football
stadium after a match?
Because all the fans have left.

Where do pirates go on holiday?
Arrr-gentina.

What kind of underwear do
clouds wear?
Thunderwear

PERFECT PETER'S HORRID DAY

'Henry, use your fork!' said Dad.

'*I'm* using my fork,' said Peter.

'Henry, sit down!' said Mum.

'*I'm* sitting down,' said Peter.

'Henry, stop spitting!' said Dad.

'*I'm* not spitting,' said Peter.

'Henry, chew with your mouth shut!' said Mum.

'*I'm* chewing with my mouth shut,' said Peter.

'Henry, don't make a mess!' said Dad.

'*I'm* not making a mess,' said Peter.

'What?' said Mum.

Perfect Peter was not having a perfect day.

Mum and Dad are too busy yelling at Henry all the time to notice how good *I* am, thought Peter.

When was the last time Mum and Dad had said, 'Marvellous, Peter, you're using your fork!' 'Wonderful, Peter, you're sitting down!' 'Superb, Peter, you're not spitting!' 'Fabulous, Peter, you're chewing with your mouth shut!' 'Perfect, Peter, you never make a mess!'

Perfect Peter dragged himself upstairs.

Everyone just expects me to be perfect, thought Peter, as he wrote his Aunt Agnes a thank you note for the super thermal vests. It's not fair.

From downstairs came the sound of raised voices.

'Henry, get your muddy shoes off the

sofa!' yelled Dad.

'Henry, stop being so horrid!' yelled Mum.

Then Perfect Peter started to think.

What if *I* were horrid? thought Peter.

Peter's mouth dropped open. What a horrid thought! He looked around quickly, to see if anyone had noticed.

He was alone in his immaculate bedroom. No one would ever know he'd thought such a terrible thing.

But imagine being horrid. No, that would never do.

Peter finished his letter, read a few pages of his favourite magazine *Best Boy*, got into bed and turned off his light without being asked.

Imagine being horrid.

What *if* I were horrid, thought Peter. I wonder what would happen.

★

When Peter woke up the next morning, he did not dash downstairs to get breakfast ready. Instead, he lazed in bed for an extra five minutes.

When he finally got out of bed Peter did not straighten the duvet.

Nor did Peter plump his pillows.

Instead Peter looked at his tidy bedroom and had a very wicked thought.

Quickly, before he could change his mind, he took off his pyjama top and did not fold it neatly. Instead he dropped it on the floor.

Mum came in.

'Good morning, darling. You must be tired, sleeping in.'

Peter hoped Mum would notice his untidy room.

'Notice anything, Mum?' said Peter.

Mum looked around.

'No,' said Mum.

'Oh,' said Peter.

'What?' said Mum.

'I haven't made my bed,' said Peter.

'Clever you to remember it's wash day,' said Mum. She stripped the sheets and duvet cover, then swooped and picked up Peter's pyjama top.

'Thank you, dear,' said Mum. She smiled and left.

Peter frowned. Clearly, he would need to work harder at being horrid.

He looked at his beautifully arranged books.

'No!' he gasped, as a dreadful thought sneaked into his head.

Then Peter squared his shoulders. Today was his horrid day, and horrid he would be. He went up to his books and knocked them over.

'HENRY!' bellowed Dad. 'Get up this minute!'

Henry slumped past Peter's door.

Peter decided he would call Henry a horrid name.

'Hello, Ugly,' said Peter. Then he went wild and stuck out his tongue.

Henry marched into Peter's bedroom. He glared at Peter.

'What did you call me?' said Henry.

Peter screamed.

Mum ran into the room.

'Stop being horrid, Henry! Look what a mess you've made in here!'

'He called me Ugly,' said Henry.

'Of course he didn't,' said Mum.

'He did too,' said Henry.

'Peter never calls people names,' said Mum. 'Now pick up those books you knocked over.'

'I didn't knock them over,' said Henry.

'Well, who did, then, the man in the moon?' said Mum.

Henry pointed at Peter.

'He did,' said Henry.

'*Did* you, Peter?' asked Mum.

Peter wanted to be really really horrid and tell a lie. But he couldn't.

'I did it, Mum,' said Peter. Boy, would he get told off now.

'Don't be silly, of course you didn't,' said Mum. 'You're just saying that to protect Henry.'

Mum smiled at Peter and frowned at Henry.

'Now leave Peter alone and get dressed,' said Mum.

'But it's the weekend,' said Henry.

'So?' said Mum.

'But Peter's not dressed.'

'I'm sure he was just about to get dressed before you barged in,' said Mum. 'See? He's already taken his pyjama top off.'

'I don't want to get dressed,' said Peter boldly.

'You poor boy,' said Mum. 'You must be feeling ill. Pop back into bed and I'll bring your breakfast up. Just let me put some clean sheets on.'

Perfect Peter scowled a tiny scowl. Clearly, he wasn't very good at being horrid yet. He would have to try harder.

At lunch Peter ate pasta was his fingers. No one noticed.

Then Henry scooped up pasta with both fists and slurped some into his mouth.

'Henry! Use your fork!' said Dad.

Peter spat into his plate.

'Peter, are you choking?' said Dad.

Henry spat across the table.

'Henry! Stop that disgusting spitting this instant!' said Mum.

Peter chewed with his mouth open.

'Peter, is there something wrong with your teeth?' asked Mum.

Henry chomped and dribbled and gulped with his mouth as wide open as possible.

'Henry! This is your last warning. Keep your mouth shut when you eat!' shouted Dad.

Peter did not understand. Why didn't anyone notice how horrid he was? He stretched out his foot and kicked Henry under the table.

Henry kicked him back harder.

Peter shrieked.

Henry got told off. Peter got dessert.

Perfect Peter did not know what to do. No matter how hard he tried to be horrid, nothing seemed to work.

'Now boys,' said Mum, 'Grandma is coming for tea this afternoon. Please keep the house tidy and leave the chocolates alone.'

'What chocolates?' said Henry.

'Never you mind,' said Mum. 'You'll have some when Grandma gets here.'

Then Peter had a truly stupendously horrid idea. He left the table without waiting to be excused and sneaked into the sitting room.

Peter searched high. Peter searched low. Then Peter found a large box of chocolates hidden behind some books.

Peter opened the box. Then he took a tiny bite out of every single chocolate. When he found good ones with gooey chocolate fudge centres he ate them. The yucky raspberry and strawberry and lemon creams he put back.

Hee Hee, thought Peter. He felt excited. What he had done was absolutely awful. Mum and Dad were sure to notice.

Then Peter looked round the tidy sitting room. Why not mess it up a bit?

Peter grabbed a cushion from the sofa. He was just about to fling it on the floor when he heard someone sneaking into the room.

'What are you doing?' said Henry.

'Nothing, Ugly,' said Peter.

'Don't call me Ugly, Toad,' said Henry.

'Don't call me Toad, Ugly,' said Peter.

'Toad!'

'Ugly!'

'TOAD!'

'UGLY!'

Mum and Dad ran in.

'Henry!' shouted Dad. 'Stop being horrid!'

'I'm not being horrid!' said Henry. 'Peter is calling me names.'

Mum and Dad looked at each other. What was going on?

'Don't lie, Henry,' said Mum.

'I did call him a name, Mum,' said Peter. 'I called him Ugly because he is ugly. So there.'

Mum stared at Peter.

Dad stared at Peter.

Henry stared at Peter.

'If Peter did call you a name, it's because you called him one first,' said Mum. 'Now leave Peter alone.'

Mum and Dad left.

'Serves you right, Henry,' said Peter.

'You're very strange today,' said Henry.

'No I'm not,' said Peter.

'Oh yes you are,' said Henry. 'You can't fool me. Listen, want to play a trick on Grandma?'

'No!' said Peter.

Ding dong.

'Grandma's here!' called Dad.

Mum, Dad, Henry, Peter and Grandma sat down together in the sitting room.

'Let me take your bag, Grandma,'
said Henry sweetly.

'Thank you dear,' said Grandma.

When no one was looking Henry
took Grandma's glasses out of her
bag and hid them behind Peter's
cushion.

Mum and Dad passed around tea
and home-made biscuits on the best
china plates.

Peter sat on the edge of the sofa
and held his breath. Any second now
Mum would get out the box of half-
eaten chocolates.

Mum stood up and got the box.

'Peter, would you like to pass round
the chocolates?' said Mum.

'Okay,' said Peter. His knees felt
wobbly. Everyone was about to find
out what a horrid thing he had done.

Peter held out the box.

'Would you like a chocolate, Mum?' said Peter. His heart pounded.

'No thanks,' said Mum.

'What about me?' said Henry.

'Would you like a chocolate, Dad?' said Peter. His hands shook.

'No thanks,' said Dad.

'What about me!' said Henry.

'Shh, Henry,' said Mum. 'Don't be so rude.'

'Would you like a chocolate, Grandma?' said Peter.

There was no escape now. Grandma loved chocolates.

'Yes, please!' said Grandma. She peered closely into the box. 'Let me see, what shall I choose? Now, where are my specs?'

Grandma reached into her bag and fumbled about.

'That's funny,' said Grandma. 'I was sure I'd brought them. Never mind.'

Grandma reached into the box, chose a chocolate and popped it into her mouth.

'Oh,' said Grandma. 'Strawberry cream. Go on Peter, have a chocolate.'

'No thanks,' said Peter.

'WHAT ABOUT ME!' screamed Horrid Henry.

'None for you,' said Dad. 'That's not how you ask.'

Peter gritted his teeth. If no one was going to notice the chewed chocolates, he'd have to do it himself.

'I will have a chocolate,' announced Peter loudly. 'Hey! Who's eaten all the fudge ones? And who's taken bites out of the rest?'

'Henry!' yelled Mum. 'I've told you
a million times to leave the chocolates
alone!'

'It wasn't me!' said Henry. 'It was Peter!'

'Stop blaming Peter,' said Dad. 'You
know he never eats sweets.'

'It's not fair!' shrieked Henry. Then
he snatched the box from Peter. 'I want
some CHOCOLATES!'

Peter snatched it back. The open
box fell to the floor. Chocolates flew
everywhere.

'HENRY, GO TO YOUR ROOM!'
yelled Mum.

'IT'S NOT FAIR!' screeched Henry.
'I'll get you for this, Peter!'

Then Horrid Henry ran out of the
room, slamming the door behind him.

Grandma patted the sofa beside her.
Peter sat down. He could not believe
it. What did a boy have to do to get
noticed?

'How's my best boy?' asked
Grandma.

Peter sighed.

Grandma gave him a big hug. 'You're
the best boy in the world, Peter, did
you know that?'

Peter glowed. Grandma was right!
He was the best.

But wait. Today he was horrid.

NO! He was perfect. His horrid day
was over.

He was much happier being perfect, anyway. Being horrid was horrible.

I've had my horrid day, thought Peter. Now I can be perfect again.

What a marvellous idea. Peter smiled and leaned back against the cushion.

CRUNCH!

'Oh dear,' said Grandma. 'That sounds like my specs. I wonder how they got there.'

Mum looked at Peter.

Dad looked at Peter.

'It wasn't me!' said Peter.

'Of course not,' said Grandma. 'I must have dropped them. Silly me.'

'Hmmm,' said Dad.

Perfect Peter ran into the kitchen and looked about. Now that I'm perfect again, what good deeds can I do? he thought.

Then Peter noticed all the dirty tea
cups and plates piled up on the worktop.
He had never done the washing up all by
himself before. Mum and Dad would be
so pleased.

Peter carefully washed and dried all the
dishes.

Then he stacked them up and carried
them to the cupboard.

'BOOOOOOO!' shrieked Horrid
Henry, leaping out from behind the door.
CRASH!

Henry vanished.

Mum and Dad ran in.

The best china lay in pieces all over the floor.

'PETER!!!' yelled Mum and Dad.

'YOU HORRID BOY!' yelled Mum.

'GO TO YOUR ROOM!' yelled Dad.

'But ... but ...' gasped Peter.

'NO BUTS!' shouted Mum. 'GO! Oh, my lovely dishes!'

Perfect Peter ran to his room.

'AHHHHHHHHHHHH!' shrieked Peter.

Henry's Summer Howlers

What happened when
Henry tied Peter's
shoelaces together?
He went on a trip.

Why can elephants swim in the
sea whenever they want?
*They always have their trunks
with them.*

Why did the banana
cover herself in
suncream?
It was peely hot.

HORRiD HENRY'S BAKE OFF

THWACK!
THWACK!
THWACK!
Moody Margaret thwacked the wall with a stick.

Why oh why did she have to live next door to someone as horrid as Henry?

Her club wasn't safe. Her biscuits weren't safe. And he was such a copy-cat. She'd told everyone she was making a chocolate sponge cake for the street party bake-off competition, and now

Henry was saying he was making a chocolate sponge cake.

And pretending he'd thought of it first.

Well, she'd show him. Her cake was sure to win. For once she'd have the last laugh.

Although . . .

Hmmm . . .

Maybe she could make sure of that . . .

★

A street party bake-off! Hurrah!

Horrid Henry loved baking. What could be better than choosing exactly what you wanted to eat and then cooking it exactly as you liked it? With loads of extra sugar and lashings of icing?

Horrid Henry loved making fudge. Horrid Henry loved making brownies. Horrid Henry loved baking chocolate cakes.

His parents, unfortunately, only liked him to make horrible food. Pizzas ruined with vegetable toppings. Sloppy gloppy porridge. And if they ever let him make muffins, they had to be wholesome muffins. With wholemeal flour. And bananas.

Ugggh.

But today, no one could stop him. It was a cake baking contest. And what a cake he'd make. His chocolate sponge cake with extra icing was guaranteed to win. He'd heard that copy-cat Margaret was making one too. Let old frog face try. No one could out-bake Chef Henry.

Plus, the winner would get their picture in the paper, AND be on

129

TV, because the famous
pastry chef Cherry
Berry was coming to
judge.
Whoopee!
Everyone
in Henry's
class was
taking part.
Too
bad, losers,
thought Horrid
Henry, dashing to the
kitchen. Chef Henry is in
the room.

Unfortunately, someone else was too.
Perfect Peter was wearing a Daffy
Daisy apron and peering anxiously at
the oven while Mum took out a baking
tray laden with mysterious grey globs.

'Out of my way, worm,' said Henry.

'I've made cupcakes for the bake-off,' said Peter. 'Look.'

Perfect Peter proudly pointed to the plate covered in lumpy blobs. His name was written on a flag poking out of one cupcake.

'Those aren't cupcakes,' said Henry. 'They're lopsided cowpats.'

'Mum,' wailed Peter. 'Henry called my cupcakes cowpats.'

'Don't be horrid, Henry,' said Mum. 'Peter, I think your cupcakes look— lovely.'

'Plopcakes more like,' said Henry.

'MUM!' screamed Peter. 'Henry said plopcakes.'

'Stop it Henry,' said Mum.

Tee hee.

All the better for him. No need to worry about Peter's saggy disasters winning.

His real competition was Margaret. Henry hated to admit it, but she was almost as good a chef as he was. Well, no way was she beating him today. Her copy-cat chocolate sponge cake wouldn't be a patch on his.

'Henry. Peter. Come out and help hang up the bunting and get cloths on the tables,' said Dad. 'The street party starts at 2 o'clock.'

'But I have to bake my cake,' yelped Henry, weighing the sugar and

chocolate. He always put in extra.

'There's plenty of time,' said Mum. 'But I need you to help me now.'

★

Moody Margaret sneaked through the back door into Henry's kitchen. She'd waited until she'd seen Henry and his family go outside to help set up the tables.

If she was too late and his cake was already baking, she could open the oven door and stomp to make Henry's sponge collapse. Or she could turn the temperature way up high, or scoop out the middle, or—

Margaret sniffed.

She couldn't smell anything baking.

What a bit of luck.

There were all Henry's ingredients on the counter, measured out and waiting to be used.

Snatch!

Moody Margaret grabbed the sugar jar and emptied it into the bin. Then she re-filled it with salt.

Tee hee, thought Moody Margaret. Wouldn't it be wonderful to pay Henry back?

'What are you doing here?' came a little voice.

Oops.

Moody Margaret whirled round.

'What are you doing here?' said Margaret.

'I live here,' said Peter.

134

'I must have come into the wrong house,' said Margaret. 'How silly of me.'

'Out of my way, worm,' came Henry's horrible voice as he slammed the front door.

'Byeeee,' said Margaret, as she skedaddled out of the back door.

Phew.

Revenge was sweet, she thought happily. Or in this case, salty.

Should he tell Henry that Margaret had come over?

No, thought Peter. Henry called my cupcakes plopcakes.

★

Horrid Henry proudly stuck his name flag in his fabulous cake.

What a triumph.

His glorious chocolate sponge, drowning in luscious icing, was definitely his best ever.

He was sure to win. He was absolutely sure to win. Just wait till Cherry Berry tried a mouthful of his cake. He'd be offered his own TV baking programme. He'd write his own cookbook. But instead of horrible recipes like 10 ways to cook broccoli – as if that would make any difference to how yucky it was – he'd have recipes for things kids actually liked to eat instead of what their parents wanted them to eat.

Chips

Chocolate worms

Frosty Freeze Ice-cream

Veg-free cheese pizza. He'd write: 'Take wrapping off pizza. Put in oven. Or, if you are feeling lazy, ring Pizza Delivery to skip the boring unwrapping and putting in oven bit.'

Yes! He'd add a few recipes with

ketchup, then sit back and count the dough.

Horrid Henry sighed happily. Didn't that icing look yummalicious. He'd left loads in the bowl, and more on the spoon. Oh boy, chocolate here I come, thought Horrid Henry. Chefs always taste their own food, don't they, he thought, shoving a huge succulent spoonful into his mouth and—

**BLECCCCCHHHHHH.
YUCK**

AAAARRRRGGGGHH.

Horrid Henry gagged.

Ugh.

He spat it out, gasping and choking.

Ugh.

It tasted worse than anything he'd ever tasted in his life. It was horrible. Disgusting. Revolting. Worse than sprouts.

So bitter. So salty.

Horrid Henry choked down some water.

How was it possible? What could he have done?

He'd been so careful, measuring out the ingredients. How could a teaspoon of salt have got into his icing?

But this wasn't even a teaspoon.

This was a bucket load.

There was only one explanation . . .

Sabotage.

Peter must have done it, in revenge
for Henry calling his cupcakes cowpats.

Wait till I get my hands on you,
Peter, you'll be sorry, you wormy worm
toad—

Wait.

Horrid Henry paused.

Was Perfect Peter evil enough to have
come up with such a dastardly plan?

No.

Was he clever enough?

No.

It had to be someone so vile, so sly, so
despicable, they would sabotage a cake.

There was only one person he knew who fitted that description.

Margaret.

Well, he'd show her.

ROOT A TOOT!
ROOT A TOOT!
ROOT A TOOT TOOT TOOT!

Margaret was blasting away on her trumpet. Blasting what she thought was a victory tune.

Not this time, frog face, thought Horrid Henry, sneaking into Moody Margaret's kitchen.

There was her chocolate sponge cake, resting proudly on a flowery china stand. What luck she'd copied him.

Whisk!

Henry snatched Margaret's cake.

Switch!

Henry plopped his salt cake on the cake stand instead.

Swap!

He stuck the name flag Margaret into his old cake.

Then he sneaked back home, clutching his stolen one.

★

Horrid Henry placed his name flag in Margaret's cake and stood back.

He had to admit, Margaret's cake was gorgeous. So chocolatey. So springy. So much chocolate icing whirling and swirling in thick globs.

Margaret was a moody old grouch, but she certainly knew how to bake a cake.

It looked good enough to eat.

And then suddenly Horrid Henry had a horrible thought.

What if Margaret had baked a decoy cake, made with soap powder instead of flour, and left it out to tempt him to steal it? Margaret was so evil, it would be just like her to come up with such a cunning plan.

Don't let her fool you twice, screeched Henry's tummy.

He'd better take the teensiest bite, just to make sure. He'd cover up the hole with icing, no problem.

Horrid Henry took a tiny bite from the back.

Oh my.

Chocolate heaven.

This cake was great.

Wow.

But what if she'd put some bad bits in the middle? He'd better take another small bite just to check. He wouldn't want Cherry Berry to be poisoned, would he?

Chomp
Chomp
Chomp.

Horrid Henry stopped chewing.

Where had that huge hole in the  cake come from? He couldn't have—

Yikes.

What was he thinking?

There was only one thing to do. He had to fill the hole fast. If he covered it with icing no one would ever know.

What could he fill the cake with to disguise the missing piece?

Newspaper?

Nah. Too bumpy.

Rice?

Too bitty.

Horrid Henry looked wildly around the kitchen.

Aha.

A sponge. A sponge for a sponge cake.

He was a genius.

Quickly Horrid Henry cut the sponge to fit the hole, slipped it inside, and covered the joins with more icing.

Perfect.

No one would ever know.

Mum came into the kitchen.

'Hurry up Henry, and bring your cake out. It's street party time.'

Horrid Henry had a brilliant time at the street party. Everyone was there. Magic Martha did magic tricks in the corner. Jazzy Jim banged on his keyboard.

145

Singing Soraya warbled behind the
bouncy castle. Jolly Josh showed off his
tap dancing.

Even Margaret
playing solo
trumpet and
Perfect Peter
singing with his band,
The Golden Goodies,
couldn't ruin Henry's
mood. He'd eyed the
other contestants as
they carried their
entries to the bake-
off table. Rude
Ralph had brought
burnt brownies.

146

Sour Susan had made horrible looking
gingerbread. Greedy Graham had
made a tottering tower of sweets with
Chocolate Hairballs, Foam Teeth,
Belcher-Squelchers and Blobby-Gobbers.

Then there were Peter's lopsided lumpies.

And Allergic Alice's gluten-free-nut-free-sugar-free-flour-free-dairy-free-beetroot-rice-cake.

Taste-free too, thought Horrid Henry.

And a rag-tag collection of droopy cakes and wobbly pies.

'Wah,' wailed Weepy William. 'I dropped mine.'

Horrid Henry and Moody Margaret shoved through the crowd as the famous judge, Cherry Berry, stood behind the cake table.

Henry had made sure his cake was at the front.

Margaret had also made sure her cake was at the front.

The two chocolate sponges faced each other.

'Nah Nah Ne Nah Nah, my cake is

best,' jeered Margaret.

'Nah Nah Ne Nah Nah, my cake is best,' jeered Henry.

They glared at each other.

Tee hee, thought Margaret.

Tee hee, thought Henry.

'Stand back from the cakes, you'll all get a chance to taste them soon,' said Cherry Berry.

She walked around the table, eyeing the goodies. She poked one, prodded another, sniffed a third. She walked around again. And again.

Then she stopped in front of Henry and Margaret's cakes.

Henry held his breath.

Yes!

'Now, don't these sponge cakes look lovely,' said Cherry Berry. 'So attractive. So fluffy. Ooh, I do love a light sponge,' she said, cutting a piece and taking a big bite.

'So spongy,' she choked, spitting out a piece of yellow kitchen sponge. 'Ugggghhh.'

Rats, thought Horrid Henry.

Cherry Berry checked the name on the flag.

'Henry's cake is disqualified.'

Double rats, thought Horrid Henry.

'Ha ha ha ha ha,' screeched Moody Margaret.

'The winner is . . . Margaret.'

'Yes!' shrieked Margaret.

Aaaarrrggghhhhh.

That was his cake. It was so unfair. His cake had won after all. He'd pay Margaret back—

'I'll just try a little piece before we share it with everyone,' said Cherry Berry, taking a huge bite.

'Blecccchhh!' gagged Cherry, spitting it out. 'Salt! Salt instead of sugar.'

'What?' screamed Moody Margaret.

How was it possible that salt had been sneaked into her cake?

Unless . . . unless . . .

'You put a sponge in my cake,' shouted Margaret.

'You put salt in my cake,' shouted Henry.

Horrid Henry grabbed a pie and hurled it at Margaret.

Moody Margaret grabbed a cake and hurled it at Henry.

Horrid Henry ducked.

SMACK

The gooey cake landed in Cherry Berry's face.

'Food fight!' shrieked Rude Ralph, snatching cupcakes and throwing them.

'Food fight!' screamed Greedy
Graham, pitching pies into the crowd.

'Stop it! Stop it!' shouted Mum, as whipped cream splatted on her head.

'Stop it!' shouted Dad, as a lemon tart splatted on his shirt.

Cherry Berry brushed cake from her face and pie from her hair.

'Wah,' she wailed, as cake dripped down her back. 'I have a soggy bottom.'

She staggered over to the cake table and gripped the edge.

The table was empty except for a few grey cupcakes.

'I proclaim Peter's lopsided lumpies the winner,' she gasped.

'Yippee,' squealed Perfect Peter.

'Noooooo,' howled Horrid Henry.

Henry's Summer Howlers

What do you call
a polar bear in
the tropics?
Lost!

Where do elephants go on holiday?
Tuscany.

Why did the teacher
wear sunglasses?
*Because she had such
a bright class.*

Where do wasps go
when they're hurt?
The waspital.

What do snowmen
wear on their heads
when it's hot?
Ice caps.

Knock, knock.
Who's there?
Ice cream.
Ice cream who?
Ice cream if you throw me
in cold water.

Why didn't the dog like swimming?
He was a boxer.

HORRiD HENRY'S
SUMMER
BOREDOM
BUSTERS

HELLO FROM AROUND THE WORLD

Look in the wordsearch to find out how Henry says hello from countries around the world.

A	Y	A	I	Z	S	S	R
H	R	X	L	D	N	A	U
A	S	E	X	O	B	G	O
L	S	Q	M	A	H	H	J
L	Z	Q	H	I	O	A	N
O	D	R	A	L	L	X	O
Y	E	L	A	R	N	A	B
M	N	A	Z	D	A	R	K

KALIMERA (Greece)   ALOHA (Hawaii)
BONJOUR (France)   SZIA (Hungary)
MERHABA (Turkey)   HALLO (Netherlands)
NAZDAR (Czech Republic)   HOLA (Spain)

Check the answers on page 199.

HORRID HENRY'S TOP PARENT-TAMING TIPS

Make sure the summer holidays go your way with Henry's ultimate tips for keeping nagging parents at bay.

• Never take 'no' for an answer.

• Don't forget to nag for what you want: eventually you will wear your parents down. If I can get Root-a-Toot trainers, anyone can.

• Tell your parents it's wasteful to have a TV and not to watch it.

• All computer games are educational. Remind your parents

162

that you will never
become a star fleet
commander unless
you get in lots of
practice zapping
enemy spaceships.

• Shock your parents by doing something
helpful every now and then without
being asked. They will be so stunned and
grateful that you can seize the moment
and ask for more pocket money.

• Don't be too helpful, or
you'll spoil your parents.
After all, they are your slaves
and live to serve you.

• Remember, you're the boss!

PERFECT PETER'S PERPLEXING PUZZLES

On long car journeys, Perfect Peter keeps busy with quiet pencil and paper puzzles. Here are some he drew for Henry to guess. Can you guess them too?

1. Which is the longest line? A or B?

Answer: _____

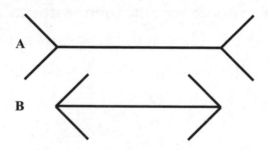

2. Which is the longest line?

A or B?

Answer: _____

3. Which is the biggest inner circle?

A or B?

Answer: _____

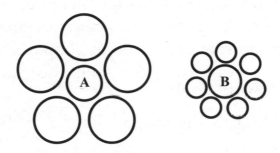

4. Which is the larger inside square?

The white square or the black square?

Answer: _____

Horrid Henry got them all wrong!

How did you do?

Check the answers on page 199.

HORRID HENRY'S NOISY CAR GAMES

Horrid Henry hates Perfect Peter's quiet car puzzles – he prefers car games that make as much noise as possible!

Henry's Noisy Animal Game

When you drive past an animal, make the noise of that animal very loudly. The loudest person gets a point, and the person to get ten points wins.

This is a brilliantly noisy game, and I'm the best player ever. Perfect Peter is rubbish.

Henry's Noisy Drumming Game

Think of a song and beat out the tune on your legs or the window. Everyone else has to guess what the song is. The person who guesses the right answer gets to be the drummer.

My new favourite band is The Smelly Bellies because they are really noisy. I always choose one of their songs.

Henry's Noisiest Game

Everyone breathes in deeply and then make a very loud noise for as long as they can. The person who can keep going the longest and the loudest is the winner.

Mum and Dad don't seem to like this game much.

SUMMER SUDOKU

Fill in the sudoku so that every square and row – both up and down – contains the four pictures shown.

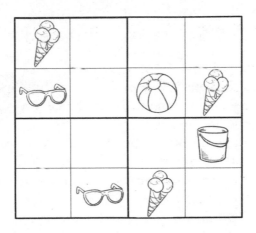

Too easy-peasy for you? Try a trickier one! Fill in every square and row with numbers 1-6.

The answers are on page 199.

		6			
	2		4	1	
	3				1
6			3	4	
	5	4		6	
			2	5	

167

HAPPY HOLiDAYS

Horrid Henry's family holidays are a disaster.
Henry's idea of a good holiday just isn't
the same as his mum and dad's. What sort
of holiday would suit you? Imagine your
dream holiday, and answer these questions.

1. **What do you dream of doing on holiday?**
(a) Going for good long walks in the countryside –
whatever the weather.
(b) Swimming in the sea, building sandcastles and
enjoying the sunshine.
(c) Sitting on the sofa, eating crisps and watching TV.

2. **What would be your perfect meal?**
(a) Sausages and baked beans cooked over an open fire.
(b) A beach barbecue and a big ice-cream.
(c) Pizza, chips, burgers, crisps, chocolate and sweets.

3. **What would you be wearing on your
dream holiday?**
(a) Walking boots, thick
socks, waterproof
trousers, woolly jumper
and an anorak.
(b) Swimming trunks or
a bikini.
(c) Pyjamas – it's a holiday!

4. **What would you
   bring back with you?**
(a) Muddy boots and
    soggy wet clothes.
(b) A collection of
    pebbles and shells.
(c) A collection of sweet wrappers and crisp packets.

5. **What are your top three tips for a
   dream holiday?**
(a) Fresh air, cold showers and quiet.
(b) Sun, sea and sand.
(c) Comfy beds, hot baths and a giant TV with
    fifty-seven channels.

ANSWERS

Mostly (a)s: Unlike Henry, you like a challenge, and your ideal
holiday is a camping trip without any home comforts. But would
you enjoy sitting in a soggy tent with the rain drip-drip-dripping
overhead? And how would you feel if you had to share your tent
with some friendly visitors – like the cows from the next-door
field?

Mostly (b)s: A traditional seaside holiday is your idea of bliss.
So pack up your swimming gear, and your bucket and spade,
and enjoy a fun-filled beach break.

Mostly (c)s: Just like Horrid Henry, your idea of a perfect holiday
would be to spend every day grossing out on pizza, chips, crisps
and sweets and watching all your favourite TV programmes.
So why go on holiday when everything you need is at home?

AEROBIC AL'S SILLY SPORTS DAY

Aerobic Al takes School Sports' Day very seriously. But he also likes organising his own Silly Sports' Day for all his friends. Here are some of his crazy races.

Air Balloons

Hand everyone a balloon, shout 'GO', and see who can keep their balloon up in the air for the longest.

Al's Rules:
• Don't catch or hold the balloon once it's up in the air.
• Never punch someone else's balloon to the ground.

Hilarious Hopping

Take two long pieces of string (same length) and lie them on the ground like a wiggly path. The two people racing have to hop along the winding string.

Al's Rules: • No pushing, shoving or tripping.

GREEDY GRAHAM'S GRUB

Greedy Graham loves ice-cream, not just in the summer, but all year round! Here's how to make your own scoop of soft vanilla ice-cream in a bag. It's easy!

Ice-cream in a bag

You will need:
Half a cup of full-fat milk
1 level tbsp sugar
1/4 tsp of vanilla essence
6 tpsps rock salt
2 self-seal sandwich bags (one inside the other)
2 large heavyweight plastic bags (one inside the other)
Lots of ice cubes (about 36)
Parcel tape

Instructions:
1. Put the ice and salt in the large bag.
2. Put the milk, vanilla essence and sugar into the small bag. Seal the bag, using parcel tape - to be extra safe!
3. Put the small bag in the large bag.
4. Gather up the top of the large bag in your hands, and shake it for about 6-7 minutes. Shake it outside or over the sink, in case of drips!
5. Open the small bag carefully, scoop out the ice-cream - and enjoy.

iCE CREAM CRiSS-CROSS

There are loads of yummy ingredients you can eat with ice-cream. Can you fit the words below into the criss-cross puzzle?

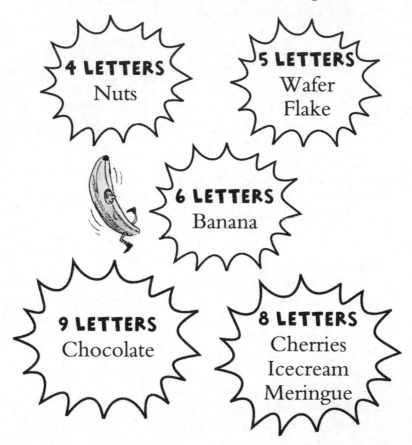

4 LETTERS
Nuts

5 LETTERS
Wafer
Flake

6 LETTERS
Banana

9 LETTERS
Chocolate

8 LETTERS
Cherries
Icecream
Meringue

12 LETTERS
Strawberries
Marshmallows

Check the answers on page 200.

SUMMER HOLIDAY WORDSEARCH

Henry's friends are all jetting off on holiday this summer. Can you find their holiday destinations in the wordsearch opposite?

BALI   ORLANDO

MIAMI

    CRETE

CORFU

    FLORIDA

EGYPT   MAJORCA

    BARBADOS

M	M	B	E	U	V	O	S
I	K	A	J	G	D	U	O
A	M	L	J	N	L	F	D
M	J	I	A	O	I	R	A
I	P	L	R	I	R	O	B
R	R	E	T	E	R	C	R
O	F	L	O	R	I	D	A
E	G	Y	P	T	Y	L	B

Go to page 200 to see the answers.

i SPY . . .

Look out of the car window and see if you
can spot something beginning with every
letter of Horrid Henry's name?
Write your answers here when you do.

H_____

O_____

R_____

R_____

I_____

D_____

H_____

E_____

N_____

R_____

Y_____

MAKE A WICKED WATERBOMB

This waterbomb is fantastic for ambushing a rival club. It's quite tricky to make at first, but it is easy once you know how.

You will need:
A square piece of paper
Water

Instructions:

1. Fold your square from corner to corner, to crease, as shown in diagram.

2. Push in the sides to create a triangle.

3. Fold up the corners to the point at the top. Turn over and repeat on the other side.

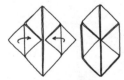

4. Fold in the sides. Turn over and repeat on the other side.

5. From the top, fold each of the flaps down and tuck into the sides, as shown. Turn over and repeat on the other side. Don't worry if they don't fit very neatly.

6. Gently pull your water bomb into shape, then blow hard into the hole at the top.

7. Fill with water – and throw very quickly!

177

BEST BEACH GAMES

Horrid Henry hates the cold sea, so if he can't escape a trip to the seaside, he gets some beach games going (then there's no time left for swimming, ha ha!)

Bury Your Little Brother or Sister

You will need:
A spade
One little brother or sister

How to play:
1. Tell your little brother to lie very still on the sand.
2. Cover him from his feet up to his neck with sand.
3. Pat it all down so he can't escape. Tee hee!

Sandcastle Contest

You will need:
2 or more players
A bucket and spade per player

How to play:
1. Mark two lines in the sand – about 20 steps apart.
2. Put the buckets and spades on one of the lines.
3. The players stand on the other line (the start line).
4. One player shouts 'GO!' The players run and collect their buckets, run back and put their buckets down on the start line, then run and get their spades.
5. Each player makes a sandcastle as quickly as possible.
6. The winner is the first person to finish their sandcastle – but if it falls apart when they remove the bucket, the second person is the winner.

HORRiD HENRY'S CAMPiNG SURVIVAL GUiDE

Horrid Henry hates family holidays,
especially camping. He'd much rather stay
at home, eating crisps and watching TV.
Here are his top survival tips.

Before You Go
- Pretend to be ill. Then
  your parents will cancel
  the holiday, and you can
  just lie on the sofa,
  under a cosy duvet and
  watch TV, while Mum
  brings you cold drinks
  and ice cream all day.

If this fails...
- Pack your suitcase very slowly. You might miss the
  train, plane or ferry, and then you'll be able to stay
  at home.
- Forget something important, like your suitcase.
  When you arrive at the campsite, your parents will
  be angry, but you'll still have to come home to get
  your bag.

- Leave your walking boots behind – by mistake, tee hee!
- Take the things you really need – like your boom-box, your Grisly Ghoul Grub Box and Dungeon Drink Kit, your Super Soaker 2000 water blaster, and lots of comics. Because camping is boring.

On The Way

- Beg your mean, horrible parents to buy a new car, with a built-in TV, fast food on tap and a jacuzzi.

If this fails...
- Sneak lots of sweets into the car.
- Hide Perfect Peter's soppy story tapes and bring your own Killer Boy Rats music.
- Tell your parents you NEED to go to the toilet – then pretend to

get locked in so that you miss your plane, train or ferry.

- Ask if you're nearly there yet – about every 10 seconds. Your parents will never want to take you on holiday again.

On Holiday

- Whine every minute of every day – it's too hot, it's too cold, the food is horrible, everything is horrible. Your parents will get so fed up, they'll take you home. Hooray!

- Do a rain dance. When it pours down and washes your tent away, you can leave the cold, horrible campsite and move to the brilliant one across the road, with its beds, hot baths and heated swimming pools.

- Hide all the disgusting healthy food your parents have brought with them so they have to take you to the nearby burger bar.

HOLIDAY HIGHLIGHTS

Horrid Henry's family, friends, and enemies
have special holiday highlights.
Untangle the names and work out
who enjoyed what.

1. Day out at a theme park **EAATGRMR**
Answer: __ __ __ __ __ __ __ __

2. Watching a football match **SMSI ELBTTA-XEA**
Answer: __ __ __ __   __ __ __ __ __ __ __ - __ __ __

3. Swimming with dolphins **GGSYO DSI**
Answer: __ __ __ __ __   __ __ __ __

4. Long lie-ins every day **DNLIA**
Answer: __ __ __ __ __

5. Trip to an ice cream factory **MGAAHR**
Answer: __ __ __ __ __ __

6. Going on a nature trail **RPTEE**
Answer: __ __ __ __ __

7. Attending the Summer School for Clever Kids
NBRAI and **EALCR**
Answer: __ __ __ __ __ __ and __ __ __ __ __

Check the answers on page 200.

CAMPSITE MAZE

Horrid Henry and his family travel on
the ferry to France, and then drive to the
campsite. But which campsite will they
arrive at – Horrid Henry's favourite,
Lazy Life, or Perfect Peter's choice?

The answers are on page 201.

PURPLE HAND HOLIDAY GAME

Take it in turns to throw the die
and draw a skull and crossbones flag.
Whose flag will be finished first?

You will need:
Two or more players
A die
Pencil and paper for each player

How to play:
1. Give each player a pencil and a piece of paper.
   Each player must draw their own skull and
   crossbones flag.
2. Take it in turns to throw the die. Throw a 6
   first to draw your flag.
3. Next, throw a 5 to draw a skull on your flag.
4. To complete your flag, you need to throw a 4
   to draw an eye (there are two eyes so you will
   need to do this twice), a 3 for the nose, a 2 for
   the mouth and a 1 for the crossbone (twice).
   You can draw these in any order – for example,
   if you get a 1 at your second go, you can add
   one of the crossbones straight away.
5. The first to complete their skull and crossbones
   flag is the WINNER.

Throw a 6 and
draw the flag.

Next, throw a
5 for the skull.

You need two 4s
for the eyes.

3 for the nose.

2 for the
mouth.

Two 1s for the
crossbones.

WINNER!

HOLIDAY HOWLERS

Match the words to these holiday jokes.
Then fit them into the criss–cross puzzle.
One word has already been filled in
to help you.

4 LETTERS
Cow
Frog
Sand

6 LETTERS
Sunday
Nobody
Monkey

5 LETTERS
Green
Sheep

7 LETTERS
Mummies
Zombies

Why did the _ _ _ _ scream?
Because the seaweed.

What's the best day to go to the beach?
_ _ _ _ _ _.

Why don't mummies go on holiday?
They are afraid they might relax and unwind.

What's _ _ _ _ _ _ and round and goes camping?
A boy sprout.

What's the best day to go to the beach?
_ _ _ _ _ _.

Why didn't the skeleton go on holiday?
He had _ _ _ _ _ _ _ _ _ _ _ to go with.

Where do _ _ _ _ _ go on holiday?
The Baa-hamas.

Where do _ _ _ _ go on holiday?
Moo-Zealand.

Why did the _ _ _ _ _ _ sunbathe?
To get an orangu-tan.

How did the _ _ _ _ cross the channel?
By hoppercraft.

Where do _ _ _ _ _ _ _ go on holiday?
The deaditerranean.

CLUE:
Fill in the
longest word
first.

M
U
M
M
I
E
S

Check the answers
on page 201.

TOP TRAVEL AGENT

Holidays. It's so important to match
the person and the place. Here's where
I'd like to send all my evil enemies
on a one-way ticket.

1. Stuck-up Steve
Steve is the world's biggest scaredy-cat. I'm sure
spending two weeks alone in the world's most
haunted house would be the holiday of a lifetime.

2. Perfect Peter
Making him a regular on
the TV show Gross-Out,
where Marvin the Maniac
would fire Goo-Shooters
at him non-stop.

3. Moody Margaret

Activity holiday swimming with sharks.
No cage required.

4. Miss Battle-Axe

Miss Battle-Axe loves history. Where better than giving her a taste of Ancient Rome?

Experience life as a Roman galley slave! You'll be rowing 24/7 for the rest of your days.

5. Bossy Bill

Bill loves bossing people around. Let's see how he does with animals. Bossy Bill, your snake-pit in the desert awaits.

6. Greasy Greta, the Demon Dinner Lady

I know Greasy Greta would enjoy a month long
FAST at a health spa where all you get to eat is
seaweed. Yum!

7. Rabid Rebecca

The Amazonian jungle, the most spider-infested
place on earth! Home of the Brazilian Wandering
Spider, the world's deadliest. Parachute her in.

TiCKETS, PLEASE!

Can you write down five places you would
send your evilest enemies on holiday?

1._____

2._____

3._____

4._____

5._____

BUBBLE TROUBLE

It's the summer holidays, and the Purple
Hand and the Secret Club are battling –
with bubbles.

**To make the
bubble mixture**

Half a cup of washing-up liquid

2 cups of water

1 tablespoon glycerine
(this is great for making the big
bubbles, but it isn't essential)

An empty plastic bottle

**These things
are also useful**

Plastic containers

Washing-up bowl

Drinking straws

How to do it

1. Mix the washing-up liquid with the water
in the plastic bottle. If you've got the glycerine,
add that too.

2. Don't shake the bottle or the mixture will be
too bubbly before you've even started!

3. Ask an adult to make bubble wands for you
out of garden wire, pipe cleaners, or to blow
really big bubbles, out of wire coat hangers.

How to make bubble wands – ADULTS ONLY!

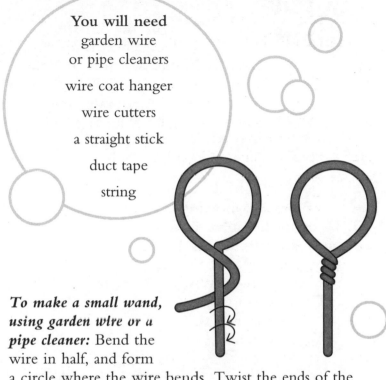

You will need
garden wire
or pipe cleaners

wire coat hanger

wire cutters

a straight stick

duct tape

string

To make a small wand, using garden wire or a pipe cleaner: Bend the wire in half, and form a circle where the wire bends. Twist the ends of the wire to form the handle. Cover any sharp ends with duct tape.

To make a large wand, using a coat hanger: Twist the hanging section into a big circle. Cut off the hooked end using the wire cutters. Fasten the stick to the twisted section of the hanger using duct tape to create a handle and to cover any sharp ends, and wrap string around it until it's secure.

Bubble Games

Bubble Bursting

Take it in turns to blow hundreds of tiny bubbles using the drinking straws and time how long it takes your rivals to burst them all.

Bubble Balancing

Using small bubble wands, blow perfect bubbles, then try to catch and balance them on your wands. The first gang to catch 10 bubbles is the winner.

Biggest Bubbles

Pour the bubble mixture into a washing-up bowl, then dip in your biggest bubble wands. The gang that can blow the biggest bubble is the winner.

CLUB GRUB

Summer means more time to
battle Margaret and her smelly
Secret Club. But can Henry
beat them to the hidden store
of sweets first?

Check the answer on page 201.

WHAT'S IN THE BAG?

Horrid Henry's holiday bag is full
of comics and sweets, but can you
guess what Perfect Peter has in his?

Across

1. Use this to draw a straight line.

4. You can write or draw with this.

6. Square and white – for blowing your nose.

7. You can borrow this from a library.

8. If you cut your knee, use one of these.

Down

2. You can use this if you make a mistake.

3. Something healthy to eat on the journey.

5. These can add colour to your work.

Check the answers on page 202.

ANSWERS

p.161

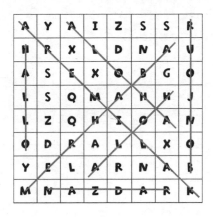

p.164–165
Did you get them right?
They are all exactly the same!

p.167

1	4	6	5	3	2
5	2	3	4	1	6
4	3	5	6	2	1
6	1	2	3	4	5
2	5	4	1	6	3
3	6	1	2	5	4

p.172-173

```
M     W A F E R
A         L
R     M B A N A N A
S     E K             C
C H E R R I E S       H
F     I               O
M     N U T S         C
E     G               O
L     U               L
L     E   I C E C R E A M
O                     T
S T R A W B E R R I E S S
```

p.174-175

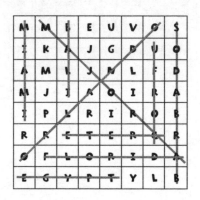

p.183

1. MARGARET
2. MISS BATTLE-AXE
3. SOGGY SID
4. LINDA
5. GRAHAM
6. PETER
7. BRIAN and CLARE

p.184–185

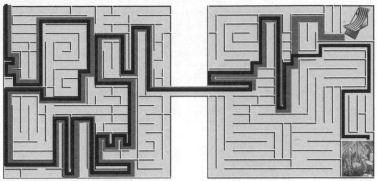

p.188–189

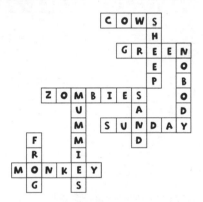

p.197

201

			¹R	U	L	E	²R
³A							U
⁴P	E	N	⁵C	I	L		B
P			R				B
L		⁶H	A	N	K	I	E
E			Y				R
		⁷B	O	O	K		
			N				
⁸P	L	A	S	T	E	R	

Visit Horrid Henry's website at
www.horridhenry.co.uk for competitions,
games, downloads and a monthly newsletter